I0757483

This book belongs to

The little girl With big feet

For my beautiful daughter, who inspires me and invites me every day to be the best version of myself. I wish you a life of plenty love, an adventure, a world where you can run free and sing loud.

And in memory of my mother, who continues to guide my steps from heaven.

This message is for you, fantastic dad or mom. You are doing a great job and doing well. Thank you so much for reading this story to your treasure.

ONCE UPON A time

It is a sunny morning
on a tiny, colourful island
in the middle of the
Pacific Ocean.

A litte girl with dark eyes and blond hair
has arrived on this planet.

She does not know that she will leave a mark on this world.

Her name is Nina.
She loves to run
during the day and
sings at night.

Nina is
very smart.
She started to walk
when she was
six months old.

Now Nina is two years old.
She can run as fast as a cheetah.

NiNa's
fiest paety shoes

Every year, Caramelito* Daycare celebrates the end
of the year with a colourful party.
There is only one rule, wear fancy shoes.

*Caramelito: lollipop in Spanish

Nina has never worn shoes.
She loves to be barefoot,
but this is a special occasion.

Nina is trying her mother's shoes.
She is so happy to get her first
pair of shoes from the shops in town.

Nina´s friend Lula come to help
her to find the best pair of shoes in town.

After visiting a few shops, Nina and Lula still haven't found the right shoes. Nina's special foot shape makes finding shoes tricky, leaving both her and Lula feeling sad.

Seeing the children's faces, Lula's mum thinks
she might be able to help.
She stays up all night knitting and cutting
leather to make a special pair of shoes for
Nina.

The next morning,
Lula's mom invites the kids for a yummy breakfast.
She asks them to close their eyes
and make a wish
.

All of them ask for the same thing:
a pair of shoes for Nina.
Lula's mum places a box
in front of the children.
All the kids opened their eyes.

When Nina opened the box, she found a card
with a message saying:

"Nothing is impossible if you really want it
from the depths of your heart".

Football Game  with mates

The Island has a few different ways to have fun!
But Nina and her mates love to play football.

Every June,
there is a championship.
The team's name is
"Tomato Sauce."

Nina has been practicing
hard all year.
She can run fast but,
waiting for the
ball is hard.

During the final match, everyone is so tired
and sad that Tomato Sauce is losing.

Nina hugs her friends and says,
"We can do it."
Tito can kick like Messi,
Mica can jump so high,
and I can run really fast.

Everyone comes back to the game with a big smile.
Nina runs past the middle of the field in a few seconds,
she passes the ball to Tito. He kicks the ball to the
corner of the soccer goal.

They start to win, and Tomato Sauce wins the match.
They are so happy, jumping, singing, and enjoying.
The Tomato Sauce team knows the most important thing
is supporting each other.

2ND

a BIG DAY

AT PRIMARY School

It is a rainy morning on the island,
it is also the first day of primary school for Nina.
She is excited and nervous for that big moment in her life.
She is waiting at home for her best friend.

Tito, who lives next door to Nina, arrives early this morning and shows his fancy pair of shoes.

Tito asks Nina where her school shoes are.

Nina frowns because she was not expecting to wear shoes at school.
She loves to be barefoot every day.

Nina's mami says "Your shoes are special.
All the children wear them, they stop your feet
from getting hurt and they make you look
nice and tidy in your new school clothes".

Nina's mami
asks her,
please check
under your bed.

When Nina looks under the bed,
she is surprised to see a box with
a fancy pair of shoes.

Nina loves them, they look so nice
and comfortable.

Tito grabs Nina's hand, and together, they walk to the school.

Class book
Maths

ABOUT US

Adri and Sofi were born in Buenos Aires, Argentina,
but the desire for adventure has taken them to New Zealand,
where, after a while, they decided to settle in Tauranga.

Adri arrived in Aotearoa in 2013 and Sofi in 2016,
the year when they both met and
began a friendship after discovering everything they had in common!

Their passion for art, their Latin roots,
and their love for New Zealand bonded them.

Adri is passionate about writing and Sofi is passionate about drawing.
They always had the dream of publishing a children's book.
And since dreams are meant to be fulfilled, they created Nina.

The Little Girl With Big Feet is their first project
together but they assure that it is not the last one!

Sofi
Adri
Nina

If you enjoyed
The Little Girl with Big Feet
and you would like to contact the author or the
artist, feel free to reach them out.

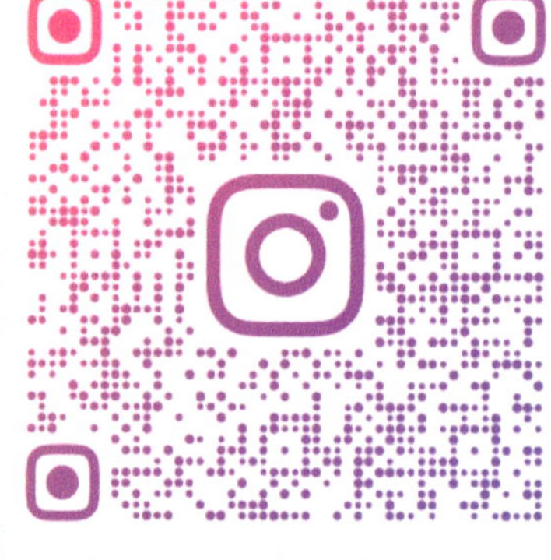

Adriana Litchfield
adriana.g.litchfield@gmail.com

Sofia Saccone
sofia.saccone@gmail.com